www.mascotbooks.com

Sully the Squirrel Explores Boston

©2016 Mark Bowers and Brian Ford. All Rights Reserved. No part of this publication may be reproduced, stored in a retrieval system or transmitted in any form by any means electronic, mechanical, or photocopying, recording or otherwise without the permission of the author.

For more information, please contact:
Mascot Books
560 Herndon Parkway #120
Herndon, VA 20170
info@mascotbooks.com

Library of Congress Control Number: 2016916368

CPSIA Code: PRT1216A
ISBN-13: 978-1-63177-635-9

Printed in the United States

Sully
THE
Squirrel

EXPLORES BOSTON

BY MARK BOWERS
AND BRIAN FORD
ILLUSTRATED BY RAYANNE VIEIRA

Sully the Squirrel lived in Boston Common, across from 84 Beacon Street, where everyone knew his name. He grew up doing things that squirrels do—climbing trees for acorns, playing with sticks, and causing mischief with his squirrel friends.

One day he noticed a red brick trail in the sidewalks and streets of Boston that lots of people followed with maps in their hands.

"I heard they call this the Freedom Trail," Sully said. He started down the path to the first site on the trail, which he learned was actually his home—the Boston Common.

"This is the oldest public park in the United States, and it's been here since 1634!" Sully said.

Sully looked up at a man taking a picture of a brick building with a gold dome and asked him, "Sir, what is that place?"

The man replied, "Hey! A talking squirrel!"

Sully shook his head and muttered, "Tourists..."

BOSTON
COMMON
FOUNDED
1634

The Freedom Trail
←

FUN FACT: Prior to the American Revolution, the Common was used as a camp for British Soldiers occupying Boston.

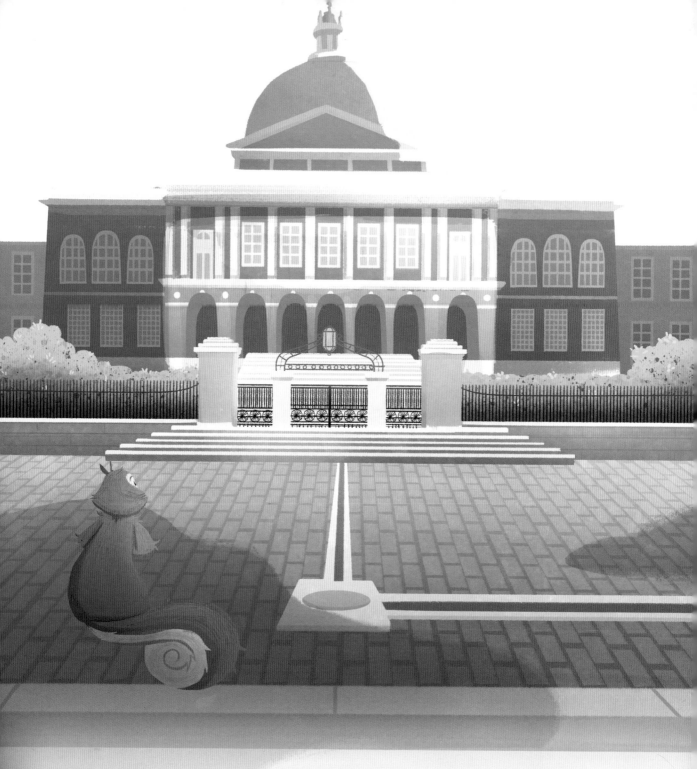

Sully climbed the stairs to the gold-domed building and entered under one of its stately arches. "It says this is the *new* Massachusetts State House, but it's over 200 years old," said Sully. He learned that a famous patriot named Paul Revere installed the copper on the dome that was later covered with a layer of actual gold. *Cool!* thought Sully.

Sully walked through a maze of hallways and found himself in the House of Representatives' Chamber, where he saw a big wooden fish hanging from the ceiling.

"Holy Mackerel!" he shouted.

A State House security guard looked down at him and said in his thick Boston accent, "Nawt in this room, pal. You'll hafta go to the Senate chaymbah to see that."

FUN FACT: The "Sacred Cod" is a carved wooden fish that was hung in the House Chamber to remind lawmakers of the importance of the Massachusetts cod fishing industry. The "Holy Mackerel" hangs in the Senate Chamber.

FUN FACT: The Old State House opened in 1713 and is one of the oldest public buildings in the US.

Sully continued on to the Old State House.

Here, on March 5, 1770, British soldiers fired their muskets upon an angry group of colonists who were armed with just snowballs. This incident became known as the Boston Massacre, which encouraged the colonists and famous patriots such as John Hancock, Samuel Adams, and Mosi Tatupu to support the idea of independence from British rule and the birth of a new nation.

From the balcony of the Old State House, the Declaration of Independence was read to Bostonians for the first time on July 18, 1776.

Sully could imagine seeing John Hancock's large signature on the legendary document all the way from the street. "I hear he signed his name so large because he wanted King George to see it without his spectacles. I guess I'll need to hold that truth as self-evident..."

Near the Old State House, Sully saw an old cemetery in the middle of a city block called the Granary Burying Grounds. *All this walking has me tired,* Sully thought. *Maybe I'll rest in the shade of one of these headstones.*

Looking for the perfect spot, he saw the headstone of a famous Bostonian, Paul Revere.

Sully also spied the graves of other great patriots.

Hey, there's Samuel Adams' and John Hancock's graves too! They signed the Declaration of Independence and played a big part in the founding of this country!

Something about seeing Sam Adams has made me thirsty. I need to find something to drink.

REVERE'S TOMB

FUN FACT: Crispus Attucks, the first casualty of the American Revolution, is buried here.

At the Bunker Hill Monument, Sully climbed all 294 steps to view the trail ahead. **"I can see all of Boston from up here!"** It was here that a small band of colonists defended the hill against invading British soldiers on June 17, 1775.

Greatly outnumbered and running low on ammunition, the colonists were famously instructed by their commanding officers, "Don't shoot until you see the whites of their eyes!" to make sure every shot counted.

It reminded Sully of the time when he picked up a pizza crust dropped by a careless tourist and was surrounded by a flock of angry seagulls—though Sully wasn't nearly as brave as the colonists. "RETREAT!" he yelled and scampered to the nearest tree.

MAP OF BOS

FUN FACT: The monument is actually on Breed's Hill.

"Ahoy there!" "Sully spied the *USS Constitution* from atop the Bunker Hill Monument. "Time for a boat ride." He scampered through the cobblestone roads of Charlestown to report for duty.

CAUTION: DIRTY WATER

The *USS Constitution* is also known as "Old Ironsides" because it is said that during battle, cannonballs would bounce off her wooden sides as if she were made of iron.

Sully spied the cannons and said, "This is the oldest commissioned ship in the entire US Naval Fleet! Let's take her out for a harbor cruise!" Sully hoisted the ship's sails but couldn't get her away from the pier. *Maybe it's out of gas*, thought Sully.

FUN FACT: The *Constitution* is currently the only active ship in the US Navy to have sunk an enemy vessel in war.

Sully darted down Union Street past the Union Oyster House (the oldest restaurant in America) and did his best to avoid the gawking tourists, duck boats, and taxicabs in this busy part of the city.

Sully found Faneuil Hall, where some of the country's Founding Fathers spoke to encourage American independence from the British Crown. This led to its nickname, the "Cradle of Liberty."

"All this history is great, but look at all the shops! And the food! I'm going to go get myself a lobster roll!" said Sully.

FUN FACT: Faneuil Hall and its marketplace is the largest tourist attraction in Boston.

FUN FACT: Paul Revere was captured but William Dawes finished the ride and successfully alerted colonists.

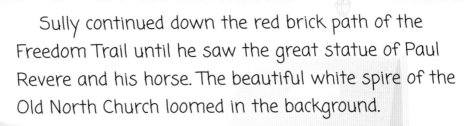

Sully continued down the red brick path of the Freedom Trail until he saw the great statue of Paul Revere and his horse. The beautiful white spire of the Old North Church loomed in the background.

On April 18, 1775, two lanterns were hung from the church's steeple to alert Paul Revere and his men which direction a British invasion would be coming from. The lanterns would be lit "one if by land, two if by sea!"

That night, one lantern was lit, and the men made their famous ride through the countryside to warn fellow colonists, "The British are coming!" The shots fired at the Battle of Lexington and Concord the next day were the first of the American Revolutionary War.

With a little tear in his eye, Sully looked up at a pair of old American soldiers dressed in Revolutionary War uniforms for a re-enactment and said, "I love you, Mass Minutemen. And obviously I'm a huge fan of the Patriots."

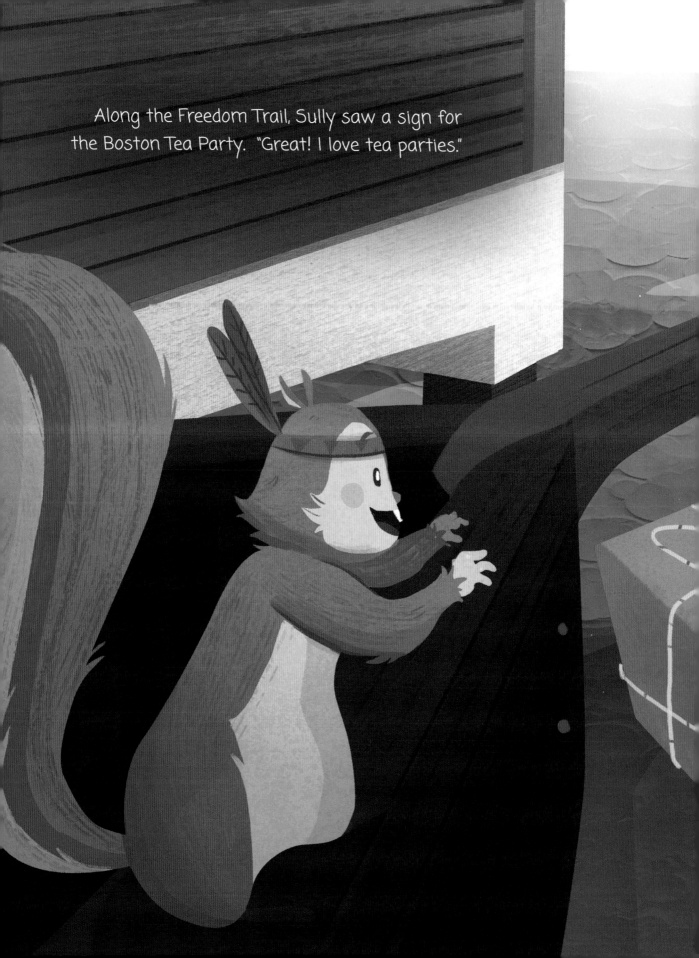

Along the Freedom Trail, Sully saw a sign for the Boston Tea Party. "Great! I love tea parties."

In 1773, Boston residents didn't like how much they were being taxed by the King of England on everyday things, like tea. A group of angry colonists disguised as Native Americans raided a ship that contained tea and destroyed its cargo by throwing it overboard into Boston Harbor. This famously became known as the Boston Tea Party. This was one of the important events that led to the start of the American Revolution.

"No taxation without representation!" hollered Sully. He was startled by a little worm that slowly moved across his little squirrel feet. "Hey! Don't tread on me!"

FUN FACT: The Boston Tea Party Ship and Museum is not located on the same site of the Tea Party itself.

On Boylston Street, Sully stepped onto a crowded sidewalk. "What are all these people doing here?" He stepped into the street and saw a bunch of humans sprinting in his direction with numbers pinned to their chests.

"The dogs must be out again! Run!" Sully ran as fast as his little legs would carry him, and he ran straight through the painted stripe on the road that said "Finish Line."

"Holy Rosie Ruiz, I think I just won the Boston Marathon!" he said as he was crowned.

Sully was given a medal, a shiny blanket, and an olive wreath to wear on his head, which he promptly ate.

4/17/2000

FUN FACT: In 1980, Rosie Ruiz is famously thought to have jumped out of the crowd and into the race at the 25.5 mile mark to claim victory.

After all that running, Sully was hungry and smelled hot roasted peanuts. He followed his nose all the way to Fenway Park, home to the Boston Red Sox.

"Welcome to Fenway Park, America's Most Beloved Ballpark," said the peanut vendor. Sully loved baseball but it made him nervous when he found out there was a Green Monster living in left field.

My Granddad told me this team was cursed for 86 years after trading Babe Ruth, the Bambino, he thought. "Monsters and curses? I'm outta here!"

Sully was tired so he hopped on the "T," America's first subway system, and headed back home to the Boston Common.

FUN FACT: "The Green Monster" is what the left field wall is called at Fenway Park. It is over 37 feet tall.

Sully was exhausted after all that sightseeing. "I never realized everything this great city has to offer," he said.

When he walked into his house, his mother asked, "Where have you been?"

"I took a trip through history," Sully replied.

"Well I'm glad you finally got out to see Boston. The world is full of wonderful things to see. Now go get washed up for dinner."

Sully thought, *I had a great day! I love sightseeing. Hmmm, I wonder what city I should explore next...*

About the Authors

Brian Ford works in the software industry and lives in North Attleboro, Massachusetts, with his wife, Kim and their children, Taylor and Conor. Brian has also written a Christmas book called *North Pole on the Eve*, which was published in 2015.

Mark Bowers, a first time author and Massachusetts native, enjoys spending quality time with his wonderful wife, Beth and their twin boys, Oliver and Henry.

Brian and Mark met in college in the mid-90's and twenty years later decided to put their immense writing talents and passion for history to good use. They hope this book will pay their kids' college tuition, or at least pay for a meal or two.